THE DAY IS WAITING

Pictures by Don Freeman

Words by Linda Zuckerman

What do you see when you look outside?

A pigeon

Some penguins

The world so wide

And all of the people

With something to do—

It's good to be out

To enjoy the view.

Where can you go on a fine, free day?

To New York

To London

To worlds far awa

By ship, train,

or airplane

However you ride

It's fun to go out

With your friends by your side.

What can you do with the long, lazy hours?

You can go to a concert

Or just smell the flowers

You can swim

You can sing

But whatever you do

It's good to know home

Will be waiting for you.

You will go out in joy and be led forth in peace;
the mountains and hills will burst into song before you, and all the trees of the field will clap their hands.

Isaiah 55:12

Don Freeman, the creator of *Corduroy*, was one of the most beloved and popular author/illustrators of picture books for children. At his death in 1978, he left behind hundreds of delightful sketches, drawings, and paintings, in several different media; none of these had ever been published. Lydia Freeman, Don Freeman's wife, felt that some of these might be used in another book for those children who had long been devoted fans of her husband's work.

Linda Zuckerman was a close friend and colleague of Don Freeman's. She is the author of *I Will Hold You 'Til You Sleep*, illustrated by Jon J. Muth, and a young adult novel, *A Taste For Rabbit*, a winner of the Oregon Book Award. She lives in Portland.

ZONDERKIDZ

The Day Is Waiting
Copyright © 1980 by Linda Z. Knab
Illustrations © 1980 by Roy Freeman

This book was previously published in 1980 by The Viking Press.

This title is also available as a Zondervan ebook.
Visit www.zondervan.com/ebooks.

Requests for information should be addressed to:
Zonderkidz, 3900 Sparks Drive SE, Grand Rapids, Michigan 49546

ISBN 978-0-310-74054-4

Cover and interior design: Deborah Washburn

Printed in China

14 15 16 17 18 / DSC / 21 20 19 18 17 16 15 14 13 12 11 10 9 8 7 6 5 4 3 2 1

For Lydia, Roy, and Sherry.
And for Klaus.
L.Z.K.